Frédéric Brrémaud

Federico Bertolucci

Little TAILS

In Prehistory

with
Chipper & Squizzo

Written by
Frédéric Brrémaud

Illustrated by
Federico Bertolucci

Translation by Mike Kennedy

Little Tails in Prehistory (Volume 4)
First Printing, 2017
ISBN: 978-1-942367-39-0

First published in France by Editions Clair De Lune

Names: Brrémaud, Frédéric. | Bertolucci, Federico, illustrator. | Kennedy, Mike (Graphic novelist), translator.
Title: Little tails. Volume 4, In prehistory / written by Frédéric Brrémaud ; illustrated by Federico Bertolucci ; translation by Mike Kennedy.
Other Titles: Petites histoires de la préhistoire. English | In prehistory | Little tails in prehistory
Description: [St. Louis, Missouri] : The Lion Forge, LLC, 2017. | "With Chipper & Squizzo." | Translation of: Les petites histoires de la préhistoire. | "Cubhouse, The Magnetic Collection."--Cover. | Interest age level: 5 and up. | Summary: "Chipper and Squizzo turn their cardboard box airplane into a time machine and travel to the prehistoric past to visit a world full of dinosaurs, ancient animals, and early man!"--Provided by publisher.
Identifiers: ISBN 978-1-942367-39-0
Subjects: LCSH: Puppies--Comic books, strips, etc. | Squirrels--Comic books, strips, etc. | Time travel--Comic books, strips, etc. | Dinosaurs--Comic books, strips, etc. | Animals, Fossil--Comic books, strips, etc. | Prehistoric peoples--Comic books, strips, etc. | CYAC: Dogs--Cartoons and comics. | Squirrels--Cartoons and comics. | Time travel--Cartoons and comics. | Dinosaurs--Cartoons and comics. | Prehistoric animals--Cartoons and comics. | Prehistoric peoples--Cartoons and comics. | Cartoons and comics. | LCGFT: Graphic novels. | GSAFD: Comic books, strips, etc.
Classification: LCC PN6747.B77 P48413 2017 | DDC 741.5973 [Fic]--dc23

OH, GREAT... THE CARDBOARD AIRPLANE IS ALL WET AND TORN APART. NOW HOW DO WE GET BACK HOME?

YOU JUST GOT HERE, AND ALREADY YOU'RE THINKING OF LEAVING?

?!

WELL, YOU KNOW WHAT THEY SAY: "IT'S ALWAYS SMART TO HAVE A PLAN B!" RIGHT, MISTER **ARCHEOPTERYX?**

WHOA -- A BIRD WITH TEETH? WOW!

VERY TRUE, LITTLE VISITORS FROM THE FUTURE! BUT DON'T WORRY...

...JUST GO TO THE VOLCANO, YOU'LL FIND HELP GETTING HOME THERE!

AH, YEAH, I CAN SEE IT FROM HERE!

PERFECT, I NEEDED TO STRETCH MY LEGS ANYWAY...

IS THAT A **PARASAUROLOPHUS**? BOY, HE SURE IS BIG!

HE MAY BE 30 FEET TALL, BUT HE'S ACTUALLY KIND OF SMALL! MANY PREHISTORIC ANIMALS ARE EVEN MORE ENORMOUS!

OH YEAH? WHERE ARE THEY?

WOOP--!

BOOM!

AH !

LOOK OUT!

THIS WAY! FOLLOW ME, HURRY!

TRICERATOPS ARE HERBIVORES -- THEY ONLY EAT PLANTS! THEY'RE OKAY!

EXACTLY!

HEH HEH! PROTECTED BY ANOTHER BIG ANIMAL, WE'LL BE SAFE HERE!

SORRY, PTERODACTYL!

UH... I'M NOT SO SURE! LOOK!

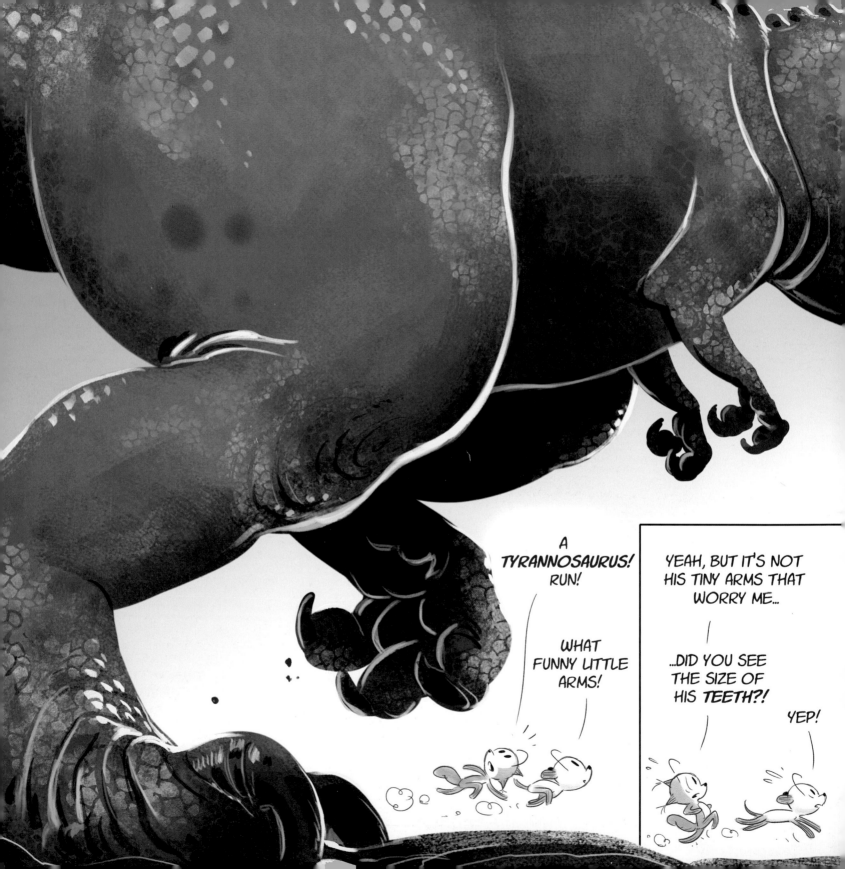

?!

BLUB...
BLLBLUB...
BLUBBLUB!

HA HA HA!
THIS ONE IS FUN!
DO YOU KNOW HIM?

YEAH, HE'S AN
ELASMOSAURUS!
YOU WANNA DIVE
AGAIN?

*LET'S
DIVE!*

PLOOF!

?!

PLOTCH! SPLATCH!

A CRO.... A CROC... ...A CROCODILE?!

NO, A KRONOSAURUS!

CLAC!

IS THAT A PREHISTORIC SLOTH OVER THERE?

IT'S A *MEGATHERIUM!* THEY COULD GROW UP TO 20 FEET LONG!

HMM...

WHAT'S WRONG? YOU LOOK WORRIED!

I'M THINKING...

THE PLATYBELODON AND THE MEGATHERIUM LIVED MILLIONS OF YEARS AFTER THE DINOSAURS HAD DISAPPEARED...!

AND YOU THINK IT'S STRANGE TO FIND THEM BOTH IN THE SAME STORY?

A LITTLE, YEAH...

OF COURSE! BY JUMPING FROM ONE ERA TO ANOTHER, IT'S EASIER TO EXPLAIN THE HISTORY OF EVOLUTION!

IF YOU SAY SO, I'M LISTENING...

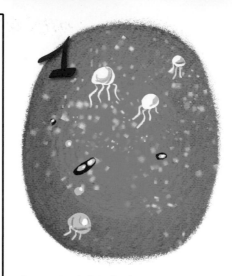

EVERYTHING STARTED IN THE OCEAN?

YEP! AFTER THE VERY FIRST TINY CELLS OF LIFE APPEARED, THEY EVOLVED INTO FISH!

THE FIRST DINOSAURS LIVED 250 MILLION YEARS AGO, AND THEY RULED THE EARTH FOR A LONG, LONG TIME. BUT THEN THEY SUDDENLY DISAPPEARED, PROBABLY BECAUSE OF A GIANT METEORITE THAT HIT THE EARTH!

AFTER THE FIRST AMPHIBIANS CRAWLED TO SHORE, THEY SLOWLY EVOLVED INTO THE FIRST REPTILES... BUT THAT TOOK MILLIONS AND MILLIONS OF YEARS!

EVENTUALLY, THE CURIOUS ONES CRAWLED OUT OF THE WATER ONTO LAND!

KINDA LIKE WE JUST DID... MAYBE THEY WERE SCARED, TOO!

YOU WEREN'T KIDDING... THIS REALLY WAS A TIME TRAVELING ADVENTURE!

YEP! FROM THE FIRST DINOSAURS TO THE FIRST MAN, IT'S ALL ONE BIG JOURNEY!

DID EVERYONE DIE? POOR THINGS...

NOT EVERYONE, FORTUNATELY! SOME BIRDS AND SMALL MAMMALS SURVIVED, AND IN TIME, THEY DEVELOPED AND GREW... AND THE CHARMING READERS OF THIS BOOK ARE THE RESULT OF THAT LONG EVOLUTION!

I CAN'T FEEL MY FEET, AND IT'S GETTING KINDA COLD... ARE WE GETTING ANY CLOSER TO THE VOLCANO?

I DON'T KNOW...

?!

HA HA HA! HE'S GOT THE BODY OF A HORSE, A LONG NECK LIKE A CAMEL, AND A TINY TRUNK LIKE AN ELEPHANT! NOW THAT'S FUNNY!

GO AHEAD, LAUGHTER WILL WARM YOU UP!

YOU'RE NOT SO BAD-LOOKING, EITHER! HEH!

HOP ON, I'LL TAKE YOU THERE!

OKAY, GIDDY-UP, SILLY-LOOKING CAMEL!

SURE! BUT I'M NOT A CAMEL -- I'M A *MACRAUCHENIA!*

IS THIS REALLY THE WAY BACK? IT'S GETTING PRETTY HOT...

YEP, PAPA AND HIS FRIENDS ARE EXPECTING YOU!

FFFSSSSHHH!

I'M STARTING TO MISS THE COLD...

?!

WHOA! WE'RE AT THE TOP OF THE VOLCANO!

GO ON, GET UP THERE BEFORE THERE'S TOO MUCH PRESSURE!

I NEVER THOUGHT I'D EVER TRAVEL ON A PRESSURE COOKER!

HAVE A SAFE TRIP!

THANKS, CRO-MAGNON KID!

WE'LL SEND YOU A POSTCARD!

HOLD ON, THIS COULD GET DANGEROUS!

YOU THINK SO?!

SSSSHHH

PLOP!

"PREHISTORY" IS A TERM USED TO DESCRIBE THE PERIOD OF TIME BETWEEN THE FIRST APPEARANCE OF HUMAN BEINGS ABOUT 200,000 YEARS AGO TO WHEN THEY FIRST INVENTED WRITING. THERE ARE MANY DIFFERENT ERAS INCLUDED IN "PREHISTORY," SUCH AS **THE PALEOLITHIC ERA,** WHEN THE VERY FIRST PRIMITIVE HUMAN APPEARED, **THE MESOLITHIC ERA,** WHEN MAN STARTED USING TOOLS, AND **THE NEOLITHIC ERA,** WHEN PEOPLE STARTED TO BUILD VILLAGES TOGETHER. THE TERM IS SOMETIMES ALSO USED TO INCLUDE EVERYTHING BEFORE THE APPEARANCE OF MAN, ALL THE WAY BACK TO THE BIRTH OF THE PLANET 4.6 BILLION YEARS AGO!

DIPLODOCUS

NOT QUITE AS BIG AS THE **ARGENTINOSAURUS,** THE DIPLODOCUS WAS STILL AN AMAZING 100 FEET LONG! WHEN HE WAS THREATENED, HE COULD WHIP HIS MASSIVE TAIL THROUGH THE AIR -- ONE BLOW WOULD CERTAINLY HURT A PREDATOR, AND THE LOUD SOUND OF THE THE MOVEMENT WOULD SCARE OTHERS AWAY! AS A HERBIVORE, HE LIVED ON THE PLAINS WHERE HE WOULD MOSTLY EAT A **_LOT_** OF PLANTS AND LEAVES.

ARCHAEOPTERYX

LADIES AND GENTLEMEN! INTRODUCING WHAT WAS MOST LIKELY THE VERY FIRST BIRD IN THE WORLD! OR ONE OF THE OLDEST BIRDS, AT LEAST, APPEARING MORE THAN 150 MILLION YEARS AGO. A FOSSIL WAS DISCOVERED IN GERMANY IN 1861 SHOWING THAT THIS BEAUTIFUL BIRD ACTUALLY HAD TEETH. YES, REALLY -- A BIRD WITH TEETH! CAN YOU IMAGINE IF CHICKENS HAD TEETH TODAY? THAT WOULD BE WEIRD!

PTERODACTYL

EVEN THOUGH IT MIGHT BE THE MOST FAMOUS TYPE OF *PTEROSAUR* (FLYING REPTILE), THANKS TO THE MANY FOSSILS FOUND, THE PTERODACTYL WAS ACTUALLY ABOUT THE SIZE OF A NORMAL PIGEON! ITS BIGGER BROTHER, *THE QUETZALCOATLUS*, WAS A LOT BIGGER -- ITS WINGSPAN WAS ALMOST 30 FEET ACROSS, MAKING IT THE LARGEST FLYING ANIMAL OF ALL TIME!

TYRANNOSAURUS REX →

THE MOST FAMOUS DINOSAUR, THANKS TO THE MANY MOVIES HE HAS APPEARED IN, THE TYRANNOSAURUS REX (OR "T-REX") IS CONSIDERED THE MOST DANGEROUS DINOSAUR OF ALL TIME. WITH HIS MASSIVE JAW AND BIG TEETH, HE COULD CRUSH THE BONES OF HIS PREY, EVEN THE ARMOR-HEADED *TRICERATOPS!* ACCORDING TO THE FOSSILS LEFT BEHIND, THE T-REX LIVED MOSTLY IN FORESTS AND SWAMPS.

WHERE ARE YOU GOING?

TO THE BEACH, OR MAYBE THE MOUNTAINS...

IT DOESN'T MATTER, AS LONG AS IT'S AWAY FROM THE T-REX!

ELASMOSAURUS

WHEN THE DINOSAURS RULED THE EARTH, THE *PLESIOSAURS* RULED THE OCEANS. ONE OF THOSE GIANT WATER REPTILES WAS THE ELASMOSAURUS. WHEN SCIENTISTS DISCOVERED A PART OF THEIR SKELETON IN 1868, THEY THOUGHT THEY FOUND ITS TAIL... BUT IT WAS REALLY THE NECK! THIS ALLOWED HIM TO LOOK FOR FOOD AT THE BOTTOM OF THE WATER AND KEEP AN EYE ON HIS SURROUNDINGS WHILE SWIMMING. THEY COULD GROW UP TO 50 FEET LONG, WITH UP TO 76 VERTEBRAE BONES -- THAT'S MORE THAN ANY OTHER ANIMAL EVER KNOWN!

TRICERATOPS

THIS SPECIES OF GIANT PREHISTORIC RHINOCEROS COULD WEIGH UP TO 10 TONS. THEY LIVED AT THE SAME TIME AS THE T-REX, BUT THEY ATE LEAVES AND FERNS, WHICH THEY COULD TEAR OFF TREES WITH THEIR PARROT-LIKE BEAKS. THEIR NAME MEANS "THREE-HORNED FACE," AND THEY HAD LARGE BONY COLLARS ON THE BACK OF THEIR HEAD. WHILE SOME PEOPLE THINK THAT WAS TO PROTECT THEIR NECK IN A FIGHT, OR MAYBE TO INTIMIDATE PREDATORS, IT WAS MOSTLY USED TO ATTRACT A MATE, LIKE DEER ANTLERS OR A PEACOCK'S TAIL -- AS A SIGN OF BEAUTY AND STRENGTH.

WHAT? WHAT'S SO FUNNY? WHY ARE YOU LAUGHING?

HA! HA! HA!

MAMMOTH

THE WOOLLY MAMMOTH WAS A VERY CLOSE GENETIC RELATIVE TO THE MODERN-DAY ELEPHANT, BUT THEY WERE LARGER, MOVING IN HERDS THROUGH THE COLD PLAINS OF NORTH AMERICA, EUROPE, AND ASIA, SCRAPING THE SNOW WITH THEIR LONG TUSKS IN SEARCH OF GRASS TO EAT. EVEN THOUGH THEY FIRST APPEARED ON EARTH 5 MILLION YEARS AGO, THEY DIED OUT ONLY 4,000 YEARS AGO, MOSTLY BECAUSE THEY WERE A FAVORITE HUNTING PREY FOR EARLY MAN.

CRO-MAGNON MAN

CRO-MAGNON MAN IS PROBABLY THE MOST FAMOUS OF THE "CAVEMEN." THEY LIVED IN EUROPE BETWEEN 40,000 AND 100,000 YEARS BEFORE THE AGE OF "MODERN MAN." ORIGINALLY FROM DISTANT AFRICA, THEY LIVED IN CLANS OF ABOUT 30 PEOPLE, AND THEY WOULD GATHER BERRIES, HUNT, AND FISH FOR FOOD. THEY LIVED IN CAVES (ALTHOUGH SOME OF THE SMARTER ONES FIGURED OUT HOW TO MAKE TENTS), AND THEY INVENTED THE COMIC STRIP! WELL, THEY TOLD STORIES ON CAVE WALLS USING PICTURES BECAUSE THEY DIDN'T HAVE WORDS YET, BUT IT'S THE SAME IDEA!

...ZZZ...

HE'S FINALLY ASLEEP... YOU CAN CLOSE THE BOOK NOW!